STORIES OF A

CURSED ANTIQUE

Ring Enchantments And Fairytales

MARTHA WICKHAM

About the Author

Martha has studied writing with Writer's Digest and has an associate degree in social behavioral science. She has also written poems and songs and even studied screen writing and horror. She still practices writing and likes getting writing prompts. Her favorite author is VC Andrews. She loves curling up with her cat and reading those stories.

Valinora

Norwich in 16th century Europe. A town shrouded in mystery, where the rich only got richer and the rest starved and lived miserable existences.

Here was Valinora. A young woman who inexplicably thrived where everyone else suffered from crippling misery.

Valinora was not always accomplished and charming, however. The elders of the village talked about how Valinora once belonged to the most destitute of families, unable to make ends meet.

There was a strange mystery that surrounded Valinora and everything around her. She was the only woman who had a house in her name and seemed untouched by the misery surrounding her.

People seemed to be afraid of her, almost. Despite her charming nature, no one wanted to talk to her of their own volition.

When did things change?

***

A few years ago, Valinora stumbled upon a ring... a shiny ring that she could not help but look at. Stricken from hunger and poverty, Valinora took the ring. She could sell the ring and perhaps buy a bite to eat and maybe get some new shoes.

As she walked towards the village, she realized she could not sell the ring. She knew that if she tried to sell the ring, people would think that she had stolen it. Valinora took the ring to her hut and decided to figure out what to do with it later.

That night, Valinora slept hungry and cold.

The next morning when Valinora woke she felt a little strange. She realized that the sky was as dark as the abyss, but it was only over the area where she had lived. It was sunny everywhere but at her place.

This strange occurrence could not occupy her mind for too long, however. She was hungry, and her shoes were torn. She had no money to her name, absolutely nothing that could help her survive.

She could not sell the ring, either. After taking a stroll through the town, trying to figure out what she was going to do, she decided to walk back to her hut and call it a day.

She had begged and begged, but there were no scraps for her that day. Even Alvin the baker had no heels to spare, no crumbs, no gruel, not even raw grain.

It was getting dark, darker than usual, but she was so hungry that she did not care. Her frail body was breaking, and she was tired from starving herself like that. She just entered the hut, put the ring on her finger and closed her eyes.

Hours passed when she heard a loud, thunderous crack in the sky. She quickly went outside and saw a massive gathering of clouds with winds that would remind one of Zephyrus himself. Zeus lit up the sky with blue light and during the storm there was wind and lighting everywhere.

Valinora was not really scared, at that time, she could only hope that the winds did not destroy her hut, the only shelter she had.

Valinora looked at the clouds coming in and decided to go back in the hut and just gather whatever she could. After all, she might be entirely homeless in a matter of seconds, and she had to do something to protect herself from the storm.

The ring was still on her finger. She was trying to gather everything she had in the hut when she heard a loud crack outside and saw a tree explode into a ball of fire.

Valinora decided to pray for this storm to go away. Pray for one last chance, even though she had nothing worth living for, at least not in this life.

Valinora looked at the ring, then looked at the tattered and torn state of her hut and her belongings and wished all of it would just stop as tears rolled down her cheeks.

Suddenly, everything went quiet around her and the sky lit up as if Zeus himself paid a visit to stop the calamity from happening.

Valinora could not believe what had just happened. For some reason, the sky was now clear, and her hut was intact. She was relieved to know that she was safe, at least for tonight. She still had no idea what was going to happen in the coming days, but at least at the moment, things made sense.

She quickly ran back inside her hut and everything was as if it weren't even touched. Valinora spent a moment in disbelief because she was not sure what was happening in the first place.

She looked at the ring on her finger and for some reason, it was shining brighter than the sun and at that moment, she started to realize that the ring might be enchanted and maybe she could use it to turn things around.

However, Valinora was aware of the fact that the village did not take kindly to magic. Especially if women were dabbling in it.

The stakes were high, but she also knew that she had to do something as living in poverty was not going to get her anywhere.

Valinora decided to use the ring, but she started slow. Instead of wishing for anything drastic, she asked for a small hut but in a better condition and some provisions so she could eat without having to starve herself.

The wishes she made after discovering what the ring could do were so minor that it barely attracted any attention, and at the same time, it granted Valinora all the things that she needed.

Once Valinora got her wishes granted and had enough food to last her a few days and a moderately comfortable hut, she decided it was time to figure out just what the ring could do.

Valinora loved reading, despite her impoverished state, she managed to learn enough until she could read and write professionally.

Valinora wished for a donkey, so she could travel to the library. She did not wish for a horse because she knew that it would attract too much attention. Every day, she would visit the town library and spend hours there trying to figure out the origins of the ring or literature on magic that could grant wishes.

She only came across a few pieces of obscure scribbles that did talk about magic and enchantments but there was not enough to formulate something concrete and something that could give her a lead on what exactly this ring was capable of.

Valinora did not stop there, however. She decided that she was going to continue her quest and figure out what the ring was capable of because she did not trust something so powerful without having the knowledge of what it could do.

Days passed and people started noticing how a raggedy woman who once looked so malnourished started dressing nicely, looked healthy, and had a smile on her face that would never go away.

People started talking about Valinora, and some were bewitched by how beautiful, healthy, and accomplished she had become. But a lot of prying eyes started speculating something nefarious was in play. As Valinora prospered, she became more beautiful, attracting a lot more attention than she would normally.

Time was passing fast, and Europe was moving towards progress. The only person who was steadfast and still thriving happened to be Valinora.

No one knew how she managed to maintain herself, and only got richer with passing time, but people always wondered about this.

However, despite everything working in Valinora's favor, there were some suspicions that were being raised by those who would see a seemingly rich woman in a place that was stricken by severe poverty.

Valinora always had an affinity for literature and a deep love for it. She did not know where it came from, but it was there. Throughout her life, the one thing that was constant was her wish to read and perhaps someday write as well.

Being in possession of the ring, she decided that it was time to get better at writing and have all the things that she needed to get started and create a new life for herself. She even used the ring so she could get into school for free and get a formal education.

Valinora sat down and started writing a book, a book that would chronicle all her life, something that she had wanted to do for the longest time. A book that would talk about her struggle with poverty and how she survived.

It did not take her long to write the book – she was driven, and she knew she wanted to finish the book as well. After she was done writing, getting the book published was a harder task for her. The reason was simple – publications were not really kind to women of higher status or women in general.

Still, through her charm, wit, and of course, the ring, Valinora managed to get her book published and as expected, it was acclaimed across Europe. However, this acclamation did not come without a cost.

You see, while most of the women hauled Valinora as the woman who was about to bring a change in the world and make things better, a group of zealots started doubting her for dabbling in witchcraft and magic.

The conversation started spreading like wildfire, and although many of the progressive folk were under the impression that it was all just hearsay, not a lot of people took kindly to successful and accomplished women.

When the word reached Valinora, she did not pay attention to it. However, the same greed and lust were something that was slowly eating her away and was going to be her doom, as well.

Valinora decided to leave her home and belongings and decided to travel – after all, no one would recognize her if she just decided to go live somewhere else.

The day she was planning on leaving her home behind, she stepped out to find a mob right outside her estate. They were angry; had torches, chains, and pikes. They knew who they wanted, and she was standing right in front of them.

Valinora looked around, trying to figure out an exit but before she could do something, a man grabbed her by the wrists, put a bag on her face, and threw her on the floor.

Before she could even utter a word to the ring, the mob attacked her right on the spot, not giving her a chance to breathe or even defend herself.

When she finally regained consciousness, they removed the bag from her head and began tying her to a wood steak. She trembled. This was no way to die. She began to plea, "Please, I was starving." It wasn't helping. A man with large eyes looked up at her and then kept tying. When he wandered behind her, she twisted her ring with her thumb and said, "I wish I wasn't here."

Surrounded by smoke, she thought it was over, but her arms were free and as the smoke cleared, she noticed she was in an unknown vast land. She could see sheep and cows in the distance. A knight was riding her way quickly on a black horse. He approached her. "Are you stranded, my lady?"

"It's true. I don't know where I am. My name's Valinora of Bath."

"There is a ship headed that way. I can take you." He would do anything for this fair maiden. Her thick hair flowed all the way down her back and her eyes shone as black as coal. Every time she made a wish her hair would grow.

Valinora didn't want to go back but said nothing when she saw his handsome face more. "That would be wonderful."

He helped her onto the back of his horse. The large gemstones she wore would give her plenty of money when she sold them. The horse turned around. "May we stop at the marketplace first? I surely don't need all these jewels. I should like to sell."

"Of course." He nodded and they were off to his castle.

Arriving he wanted them to have lunch. She agreed to pursue him and another wish. When he left, she whispered to it, "I want to get a million pounds for this jewelry."

There was a sparkle from the diamond and a huge poof of smoke behind her. It made her jump and then she saw it. Three large piles of money. Looking at her neck and wrists, she noticed the huge gemstones were gone! Rubies, emeralds, and sapphires just vanished into thin air.

Now she needed to be able to explain it and get rid of the ring. It almost killed her. She took the bags of money and hid them behind bales of hay.

"Lunch is ready," the knight told her. "I am Benjamin, by the way. Where is your jewelry?"

"I sold it. Some ladies passing by admired it, so I sold it."

He could only accept the statement. "All right." He wanted to head towards the dining hall.

"I'll be right there."

When he left, she whispered to the ring, "I wish I didn't have this ring." It vanished and pleased, she went to lunch.

It had supplied her with more than enough money. Her life truly was prosperous. At the time she was the fairest in the land.

Fifty miles away, where small children played in a beautiful country land, there was a diamond ring shining at the bottom of a stream. Calla lilies lined the water and children laughed nearby.

It would strike again.

Ring Plantation

Back in the glory of 1875, Dutch was up in the mountains trying to find a piece of land where he and John could set up camp while John was scouting the area. It was the coldest night that they had encountered, and there were no signs of life around them. The only things they could hear were crickets, insects, and fireflies around them but that was about it; the night felt like they were the only ones on the entire earth.

John called Dutch out numerous times to see if he found something, but the only thing he could hear was his own voice echoing. But John did not give up. It took him twenty attempts to finally get a sign – the sound of Dutch running down the mountain, scared for his life. It almost seemed like he had seen a ghost, but ghosts are not real, and John knew that all too well.

Dutch ran down as quickly as he could, panting and barely standing. He pointed towards the mountain. A strange glow was emitting from the top of the mountain.

Both men had never seen anything like that before. They were curious because it was strange.

John thought to himself that this might as well be a path leading to El Dorado. "But that is just a myth," he said to himself as he walked towards Blaze, his trusty steed. He took out a pair of binoculars.

After examining the glow originating from the top of the mountain, he turned to Dutch, dumbfounded out of his mind.

They were curious, and John was aware that Dutch was afraid of ghosts. The object did have a ghostly glow to it and they were all by themselves in a vast prairie land, defenseless against ghosts. Just how exactly would they defend themselves? A gun could only help them against the living.

"We have to go up and check," John muttered as he started anxiously preparing for the climb up the mountain. Dutch, still trying to compose himself, looked toward John and gave a nod. Both men started the trek.

The night sky was as dark as death's eye, with the glow from the mountain being the only source of light. The men gathered whatever they could get their hands on and began their trek to the mountain. They did not know what they would find up there, and it was frightening – and exciting. John kept his gun in case a threat emerged.

There was only a glimmer of hope that they might find some treasure that would make them rich beyond their wildest dreams. Driven by the sheer will and greed to get rich, they defied all odds and somehow managed to keep their trek going for the better part of the night.

After a gruesome five hours, John ad Dutch finally made their way to the top and ran towards the light that was coming from a small crevice. They looked at each other and started walking towards the light; they were still terrified but there was intrigue that shrouded their judgment.

Dutch extended his hand into the crevice and tried to get a feel of whatever the glowing object was and pulled it out.

It was a ring.

Dutch turned to John and said, "A damn ring... a damn ring, John. What are we going to do with it?"

John shrugged and tried his best to hide the disappointment on his face. He took the ring from Dutch and put it on his middle finger. It fit well. He thought to himself that he would just sell it off to the highest bidder once they were out of the wilderness.

The sky was still dark and both men decided to set up camp there in the clearing, with John still wearing the ring.

"For once, I wish things could be better. This life on constant run from the law is breaking my spirit," he said as he rolled over and fell asleep, all the tiredness breaking his body.

The next morning Dutch woke John out of his sleep and excitedly told him how he found a ranch nearby and it was seemingly empty. This was him signaling that it was time to move on and finally find a place where they both could rest before they started their journey.

John, still tired from last night's trek, looked at Dutch with confusion and slowly got up. Dutch was not lying, there really was a ranch there. John gazed at Dutch, looked at the ring he was wearing, and simply nodded.
It was time for them to start heading toward the ranch. They still were not sure if the ranch was empty as it seemed. But regardless, they kept going, only hoping and wishing that their pursuit of a normal life would come to fruition.

The path to the ranch took them a day to complete, and while they were tired, they had to keep going because Dutch being cunning, did not want anyone else to get there before them.

"Do you think the ranch is empty, John?" Dutch asked John and caught him staring at the ring. He ignored the question and kept riding towards the ranch.

The men finally reached the ranch at night and to their surprise, it was deserted, with just a little cabin that could barely fit more than three people. Dutch and John decided that they would spend the night in that cabin and then explore the ranch in the morning to see the possibilities of settling here.

The next morning John woke up and decided to roam around the area, trying to figure out where they were and whether the ranch was owned by someone or not. To his best attempts, he could not figure it out. All he knew was that this ranch was empty, ready to be claimed.

John sat down and started writing in his journal about what he wished to do with this ranch, and how he was going to start setting it up once him and Dutch got access to some money. The ring was still on his finger, and John did not pay much attention to it.

Weeks turned into months, months turned into years, and John and Dutch managed to turn the ranch into a full-fledged plantation. They had all the riches one could imagine. However, over the course of years, Dutch noticed how John had started to develop this maddening ambition and every time they would argue about business, John would go feral, trying to explore more ways to make more money.

"More money than I can possibly need. Enough money to solve all my problems." This was the only thing that John would think about and to Dutch's surprise, John would get his hands on the money somehow. Sometimes he would rob a train, and other times he would discover hidden gold with the local miners.

To Dutch, John had succumbed to madness and every passing day, there would be more violent thoughts crossing John's mind.

Dutch never gave that ring a second glance. However, one night when they were looking around the plantation, Dutch saw John whispering something to the ring and the ring responding. He realized that there was something wrong but given John's deteriorating mental state, he did not pay much attention and just went to sleep.

The next morning, it was the same routine. John turning into a mad man and Dutch trying to figure out what needed to be done.

The final straw broke when later that day, John murdered a young woman for trying to find shelter on their plantation. As Dutch watched from afar, John yelled at her to leave and shot her twice. His face was pale, and his hair was a mess. He dragged her body into the barn, grunting loudly.

Seeing that woman die in cold blood made Dutch realize that something needed to be done. He decided to confront John that night in his room and end this madness once and for all. Dutch went back to his cabin, trying to wrap his head around what had happened.

He walked to John's room late at night and saw him whispering to the ring once again. Dutch was prepared for things to go wrong, and he knew that someone might not walk out of this altercation alive.

"What in Lord's name were you thinking when you murdered that girl? She was barely a teenager!" Dutch screamed at John while walking towards him.

John did not reply or even move. Upon coming closer, Dutch realized that his friend was not breathing at all. John was just sitting, whispering something into the ring. He put his hands on John's shoulder and the moment he did that, John looked at Dutch, his eyes as golden as the sun, and let out a thunderous scream loud enough to pierce through the eardrums and dripping with blood. The scream lasted a good minute and after that, John's body fell on the floor lifeless, his eyes still bleeding.

It took Dutch a good minute to figure out what just happened. He quickly tried to shake this fear off and saw a note on John's table. He, as horrified as he was, gathered enough courage to move close to the table, stepping around the body and picked up the note.

The note read, "*Dear Dutch, it has been years since we found this ring and our fate turned around. However, I have come to realize that although this ring gave us a lot, it also takes from the ones who use it – it takes their mind, conscience, and anything that is good in their life. I, as a man, have done some horrible things in my life but nothing has been as sinister as me using this ring. If you find this letter, that means I am already beyond saving. However, I would like you to take this ring and destroy it. It does not matter if you spend our entire fortune trying to destroy the ring, it must be done, and there is no other way around it.*

If this ring somehow remains intact, it will do nothing more than cause more damage and taking more lives. Do not, for our sake, wear that ring. Doing so will only cause you damage that you cannot even think of.

I am sorry I was not a good friend to you. I am sorry that I failed you. Please, if it is within you, forgive me because I can no longer forgive myself."

Dutch read the letter and sat down to collect himself. He was not sure what he had just witnessed but looking at John's body and then the ring, he realized that it was time. The ring needed to be destroyed at all costs.

He picked up the ring, locked down the plantation, took his trustworthy steed aptly named Blaze, and started the journey. Dutch still had no idea how he would destroy it. He thought to himself that it was *just* a ring. There was a sinister power attached to it, but it was *just* a ring.

***

Days passed since Dutch had left the plantation and he was still distraught with what had happened to John and how the ring was responsible. A part of him wanted to go ahead and try the ring for himself but he still could not get John's face out of his mind, his eyes smeared with blood and shining gold.

Dutch removed all thoughts of the ring and continued his journey. His mind and heart were set on destroying the object.

After three days of tedious riding and sleepless nights, Dutch was finally in the clearing. Nothing but mountains surrounded him. Dutch thought to himself that if he climbed the peak nearby, he would be able to destroy the ring without anyone catching a hint of what he was doing.

He slowly but steadily climbed the peak, took the ring out of the box and set it on a rock next to him. The ring was still as good as new, as if the years did not have any impact on the sheen of it.

After contemplating for some time, Dutch finally decided that he was going to smash the ring. No matter how powerful, it was still a ring, and it should be destroyed.

Dutch found the heaviest rock he could find and placed the ring on its flat surface. He smashed it as hard as he could. There was a loud, thunderous clang and the sky lit up to a point that it nearly blinded Dutch.

"What the – "he said out loud.

After a few seconds, Dutch looked at the rock where the ring was placed, and he was shocked to see the ring still intact. There was not a single scratch or a blemish on the ring. He gritted his teeth, struggled in a deep breath, took out his shotgun and shot the ring over the cliff. There was a bright yellow glow far off in the distance and Dutch shouted, "You have taken everything from me," as the ground began to shake violently.

"All these years I used to think that you were the reason we were blessed by the power instilled in you. You are nothing but a nightmare. You took John away from me. Why don't you take me, too?"

Dutch ended up slipping because of the shaking and failed to keep his composure. He lost his footing and fell. He rolled down the hill and sustained several bruises on his neck and head.

In his attempts to destroy the ring, Dutch ended up asking for death, as well. The ring claimed its victim.

There it was, Dutch's lifeless body, ready to be consumed by the vultures – an outlaw never to be found by humans and with the ring not being in sight.

No one knew where the ring went. The last person who held the ring had his lifeless body ready to be consumed by the vultures.

Who knew what the ring was going to do in the future. No one knew the malice it would cause... or who it would take next.

A Nightmare in Paris

The following story is set in 19th century Paris.

"A writer? How did you even come up with that? You have an excellent education, money, and an empire to run, all the luxuries you can imagine! And this is what you want to do? Become a writer so you can tarnish the family's name. Haven't you already done enough?"

"What exactly have I done, father? Besides expressing my wishes to become a writer and not taking up the seat next to you in your business? I went to the school you asked me to, studied as much as I could just so I could impress you and all of that resulted in what? You remained displeased with me and never really asked me what interests me."

"What interests you is none of my concern as long as you are working in the same business your family has been doing for generations. If not, you are free to leave and remember, the moment you step out of this mansion and meet one of your vagrants, you will never be able to come back here. The doors will be closed for you, and our family name will earn you no favors."

"Fine. Have it your way, just like you have all your life."

Lyam was the son of a rich French aristocrat who was disowned but was also trying to make ends meet. The time was not kind to him, and his decision to become a writer did not bode well with the rest of his family.

Despite Lyam being primed to take up the mantle as his father's right hand, he decided to pursue his writing and become better at what he was doing. However, in the 19th century, the world was already aware of countless great writers, and it was not an easy place for an up-and-comer.

Lyam, driven with passion, still left his family estate and moved into a much more modest place, hoping that he would finally be able to change his fortune and become one of the best writers of his time.

As mentioned before, time was not kind to him; everything around him was changing at a breakneck speed. However, Lyam was stuck, trying to figure out his legacy.

It was during that time he ran into a group of clochards who, much like Lyam, were against the modernization of Paris. Lyam decided that it would be best if he joined hands with them because they shared mentalities, and it really is impossible to survive in this world alone.

The group Lyam started living with was up to no good, and he was aware of that from the start. However, he just needed some company. It was also an act of rebellion against his father; he wanted to show his father that he was more than okay without the estate, business, and never-ending wealth.

Lyam and the clochards were always on the go – after all, none of them had the money to actually afford a place and no one was aware of the fact that Lyam belonged to an affluent family during that time.

Things were fine for Lyam and his group of friends. Everything looked like it was working in his favor. However, no one had the faintest idea that things were about to change drastically.

Their travels took them all over Paris and while some experiences were worth writing about in a book, not all of them were. Some experiences were terrible, and they were not sure if they were going to survive through the night. Still, Lyam was headstrong and steadfast: he decided that he was not going to abandon his pursuits to become a writer and prove the world wrong.

During their travels, the group happened upon an abandoned estate. It was deserted and had a strange feeling to it. It was almost as if something or someone of great corruption existed there. Lyam was not terrified at all; he loved places like that. So, keeping that in mind, he suggested to his friends that they set up there and stay for a few days.

After all, this place looked exactly like the ones that Lyam had imagined for his stories. It could have made the perfect setting and considering how travel-weary everyone was, stopping here to rest was not really a bad idea.

They did not have to do much of the work because the place was deserted but it did have buildings that they could just move into without worrying too much.

Everyone took their time in settling in but not Lyam – he was the only one who wanted to explore. After all, this place was just what Lyam wanted for his book, it was almost as if this place was calling for him.

Lyam grabbed a piece of rock and scraped it on the pavement to ensure that he was leaving a mark, in case he got lost while trying to explore. He kept the rock with him and left markers that would lead him back when he needed help.

The place was massive and there was no sign of life... just emptiness everywhere. However, Lyam noticed an eerie presence that lingered around that place. He looked around but could not find anything or anyone that would still be residing here.

During his exploration, Lyam reached a massive clearing that looked like it had been burned to the ground. For a second, Lyam was shocked but being a writer and someone who was well-read, he did not let any fable scare him and decided to move closer.

When Lyam moved closer, he felt this strange feeling inside his body. As if his lungs were about to collapse for reasons unknown. He was scared but also intrigued at the same time. He wanted to know more about this place, and he kept moving around to see what would happen. After all, what was the worst thing that could happen?

And then Lyam saw it... a ring, buried under the burnt wood but still glittery enough for someone to notice it. One could easily think that the ring was calling to them and maybe it was.

Lyam extended his hands towards the ring and picked it up, dusted off the ash from it, and while he was inspecting it, a strange shriek pierced through the sky, almost deafening Lyam.

Lyam unwillingly dropped to his knees, covering his ears and trying to protect his hearing from the shriek that was perhaps the loudest he could hear. The ring was also out of his hands now. The scream lasted for five minutes until one of the clochards came looking for Lyam, and the moment they set eyes on him, everything stopped.

"Hey Lyam, are you okay? We heard screams coming from everywhere and rushed here as soon as we could," one of them said.

"Yes, yes, Mel. Everything is fine. I am not sure what the sound was, but it seems to have stopped."

Lyam got up, dusted his clothes, and made sure that he still had possession of the ring. He picked up the ring and hid it in his pocket. He was very well aware of the fact that if someone got wind of it, things would get out of hand because, unlike him, everyone was in need of money, and they would sell whatever they could get their hands on.

Still trying to process what had happened, Lyam signaled to his *friend* that he was fine, and they both continued their journey back to the building they were staying in.

It was getting dark, so they made haste and returned to the building. Thankfully, the rest of the people had proved themselves useful, as well. There was food and some wine for them to enjoy.

Lyam, at first, thought that he should tell everyone about the ring, but considering how the ring was valuable, Lyam decided that it would be best if the ring was kept a secret, at least until he figured out what the ring was all about.

"I don't need the ring; I could just throw it away or give it to these people. But there is something about it that has me intrigued," he said to himself.

That night when everyone went to sleep, Lyam took out the ring to inspect it closely. It was unlike anything he ever saw, which was unusual, considering how he grew up around ornate and highly intricate jewelry all his life.

"What is up with this ring? Something tells me to just throw it away and get rid of it, but at the same time, it keeps drawing me to itself. I cannot help but look at it."

He still inspected it closely, trying to figure out the origins or at least the motifs on the ring, but he could not make sense of it. The only thing that was apparent about the ring was this gleam to it, which looked unnatural.

Still interested in knowing more about the ring, he put it on his finger and decided to sleep. It was getting late, and he was tired from all the commotion that had taken place earlier that day.

Lyam closed his eyes and started talking to himself. "I have everything I need to write a book, a good setting, a great start. All I need is a good idea, and I will be set," he said as he started to drift.

It did not take Lyam a long time to fall asleep, and while he was asleep, the ring lit up and engulfed the entire room in white, blinding light. Lyam was already fast asleep and did not really pay attention to what had happened.

When Lyam woke up the next morning, he immediately started writing on the pen and paper that he had access to at that time. His mind was rushing with ideas, and for a moment, he felt like there were just too many ideas in his head to pen them down.

"I must get everything on the paper before I forget. There are so many ideas in my mind. I need to put them down. The world will know that I am a good writer... my father will know that I have what it takes. My father..."

Everyone in the group was worried that something had bewitched Lyam, but he was acting just fine. Aside from the fact that he could not be separated from the pen and paper that he had. "Hey Lyam, are you sure you are okay? You look like you have not had any sleep. We all are worried about you," said one of the clochards.

"Oh, yes. I am fine! Nothing to worry about. Just want to get done with my writings so I can proceed and get some peaceful sleep."

He spent the entire day scribbling away on the notes that he was making. There was no coherence, one idea would only cross his mind, and the moment he would start on it, there would be another idea taking its place.

"Ideas, ideas, ideas. What do I do?"

Lyam was so immersed in writing that his fingers started cramping because of all the time he'd spent using the pen.

By the end of that day, Lyam had run out of pen and paper. When he sat down to read everything that he had written, it all made no sense. Needless to say, it was evident that Lyam had written so much, but none of it made sense.

Lyam took the writings to his friends, and they all called him crazy. Some even asked him to stop dreaming about writing because he could never be a good writer. This made him angry, and he decided to leave the camp and find solitude – someplace where he could be alone and write.

"These useless vagrants have no idea what I am capable of. I will become the greatest writer that they have had the chance to see and once I do that, I will come for all of them."

However, fate had other plans for Lyam. The next day, when he woke up, he decided to give it a try again and sat down with new pages and a fresh pen. He was determined and was not going to stop until he had the perfect story... a story that would shock the world.

Lyam started writing again, and he spent the entire day and night writing. His friends were certainly worried about him, but every time they would knock at his door, he would tell them that he would come out once the story was complete.

"Go away, please. I need to finish this story. I cannot stop the ideas from coming to me. They need to be penned down."

Two days had passed, and Lyam did not step out of the room. When his groupies started thinking about it, his sudden silence worried them even more. That night, they decided to enter his room to figure out what had happened.

To their surprise, Lyam's room was locked. This was strange because Lyam would never lock his door. He had no belongings with him, and he was never really worried about things getting stolen.

Confused, they decided to break down the door. Considering how the building was not in the best shape, breaking the door down was an easy task, and they managed to force their way in. However, what they saw inside Lyam's room shook them for life.

The room was covered in blood, with Lyam's lifeless body on the floor. On the same floor, next to Lyam's body, there were scribblings that were written in blood. Lyam's blood.

The only reason why the ceiling was not covered in blood was that Lyam was not that tall to reach the ceiling.

All of them freaked out on the spot, trying to figure out what had happened here and what made Lyam do this to himself. Why would he kill himself? No one knew; all they could see and piece together was the fact that Lyam's ambition of becoming a writer took him to the extent that no one thought he would go, not even him, perhaps.

Perhaps he had not killed himself on purpose. It seemed that Lyam had run out of ink, and instead of finding more ink, he decided to open his veins and use his own blood. He had become so obsessed about finishing his book that it consumed him until he was no more.

Lyam was dead, and his groupies could not do anything about it. Upon close inspection of his body, one of them found a ring on Lyam's hand. Before anyone would notice, he took off the ring and slid it into his own pocket.

This heinous incident was not something they could report to the authorities. After all, what would they tell them that would make sense to anyone? None of this made sense or even felt natural to them.

Confused and disturbed, the group could not figure out what to do. The entire room and Lyam's body were nothing more than a grotesque scene that looked like a crime that only a heinous monster could commit, yet they knew it was Lyam who did this.

After some time, they decided that the best thing that they could do was set the entire room on fire with Lyam's body in it and then run away from that place, never to be seen again.

They gathered what they would need plus some fuel and set everything on fire. The room was small, and the fire spread like anything. It only took a few minutes for the fire to engulf and destroy everything in its way.

By the time the fire caught the rest of the building, Lyam's body was nothing but ash, and the group had run away with whatever they could get their hands on... including the ring.

A Cursed Antique

"Jimmy, darling, it is time to wake up. You have been sleeping late and it is not going to help you build your dreams."

Rachel was tired of her son Jimmy being lazy all over again. He was a bright young kid who had the world at his feet, but he would still spend his time sleeping and getting bad grades in school.

What was the problem? Well, Jimmy did not care much about his grades or anything else, for all that matter. He did not care about building a future. Much rather, he was interested in exploring the unknown and taking one day at a time.

His mother, Rachel, on the other hand, was much more ambitious. Being a single mother and in charge of a household, she had to make sure that Jimmy was doing good in all aspects of life.

"Mom, it's the weekend. I'm supposed to sleep till late!" Jimmy sighed and spoke while half asleep. His room was locked, and despite Rachel's incessant knocking, he did not get up to open the door.

"How many times do I have to tell you that you are not to lock your room on the weekends? I have to come in early and get the laundry and you, my handsome prince, never wake up on time," Rachel yelled through the door, frustrated and tired.

"You know what, stay asleep as long as you want," she exclaimed, giving up. "I have to go to the airport to pick up your grandfather.

His flight lands in an hour. When I return, I expect you and your room to be clean."

Rachel left with that warning, despite knowing very well that she would not do anything if he failed to listen.

Rachel's father was returning from his trip to Paris, and even though he was old, he did not let age get in his way and his activities. A lot of people would tell him that he was living on borrowed time, but Mike was as young as they come. Looking at Mike, one could almost mistake him for someone who is in their early 30s.

He was fit, active, full of life, and always loved a challenge. Traveling was one thing that he adored. Mike, from his early days, was a traveler. He went from one place to another finding new and interesting things that would not only pique his interest but also the interest of those around him. After spending years in Paris, he was finally returning to see his daughter and her son.

Rachel left in a hurry, thinking that Jimmy would take her seriously and get his act together. After all, a mother's trust is, at times, easily earned. Jimmy, on the other hand, knew that Rachel would take her time coming back, and he would only need ten minutes to get everything in order.

So, Jimmy decided to switch on his gaming console, called a few friends, and asked everyone to hop online so they could play a few rounds together. Jimmy, as well as anyone else, knew that gaming online with friends takes most of your time.

Minutes turned into hours, and Jimmy was still on his couch when he heard someone enter through the front door. He looked at the time and freaked out. Immediately, he hustled around the room to make it look presentable for when Rachel and Mike arrived.

Mike was excited to see Jimmy. "Look at you, young man. You were so young when I last saw you. Now, you can easily pass off as an adult," said Mike as he patted Jimmy on the back.

Rachel, on the other hand, was not pleased and gave Jimmy an angry look as she turned to Mike and said, "Dad, let's get you settled. We have a lot to talk about, and you must be hungry."

"Jimmy, I am going to give you another ten minutes to rethink the conversation that we had earlier this morning, or you will spend the next ten months wondering what happened to your console," Rachel warned before she took her father to his room.

Jimmy knew that this was not just an empty warning. He decided to clean his entire room and take a shower so he could look presentable. After all, he wanted to spend more time with Mike and figure out where his adventures took him this time around.

It was around ten at night when Rachel, Mike, and Jimmy gathered at the dinner table. It was takeaway night, and Mike would not have it any other way.

"So, Jimmy, what you have been up to?" Mike asked, wanting to know more about his grandson. Despite being old, he kept himself well-versed and knew what was happening around the world.

"Nothing, Grandpa. I'm just trying to figure out where to set my foot in school and where to apply. Mom wants me to study business, but I have an interest in finance. What do you think?" Jimmy said with a mouthful of food.

"Well, I would suggest that you do a bit of both. There are plenty of programs that teach you both finance and business. Allowing you to know not only how management works but also where the money comes."

Rachel was listening to the whole conversation and was content that after a long time, Jimmy was interested in talking to someone about his studies.

"College will happen in its due time. Dad, tell me what you were up to in Paris. I thought you didn't like that place at all!" said Rachel as she decided to pick up the plates with Jimmy.

"Oh honey, I still don't like Paris. But this time around, the experience was different. You see, I decided to ditch the tour guides and explored the entirety of it on my own and let me tell you ... I found so many interesting things. Most importantly, I found this."

Mike pulled out a ring from his finger and placed it right in the center of the dinner table. Rachel, for a moment, could not believe the beauty of the ring. Jimmy, on the other hand, had something else on his mind.

How can this ring be so perfect? I bet it costs a lot of money! he thought to himself as he looked at the ring with a sparkle in his eyes.

"Can I hold it, Grandpa?" said Jimmy excitedly as he moved his hand forward. Before he could even grab it, Mike picked up the ring and handed it to Jimmy to look at.

It was obvious to everyone that Jimmy was attracted to this ring more than anyone else in the room. Unlike Rachel, he wanted to know more about the ring.

Luckily for him, his grandfather was more than happy talking about the ring in detail. He decided to spill the beans about how he found it.

"I happened to find myself lost in the bustling streets of Paris when I stumbled upon this place that I'd never seen before during several of my trips in Paris. It had a few vintage watches on display, some ornate pens, and a number of cufflinks. This ring, however, was the one thing that caught my attention," said Mike as he moved towards the fridge in order to get some water for himself.

"You see, in that shop, I ran into this charming young man who was way too handsome to be running the place. I first thought that he was just filling in for someone, but he told me that he owned the place and everything he had was for sale. Except for one thing... this ring."

At this point, both Rachel and Jimmy were more than interested in finding out more and decided to spend a bit more time understanding what was happening. They kept on listening.

"I asked him what's so special about this ring, and the young man started telling me about how it was forged in the deepest pits of hell and somehow managed to make its way to earth where it has found its way to one person or another throughout the course of history."

Jimmy scoffed and said, "Come on, Grandpa. You do not expect me to believe that hell exists, and someone decided to forge this ring. The next thing you will tell us is that the man who forged this ring was Sauron."

Mike, unbothered, continued to tell the story, "Well, I picked up the ring from that young man. When I asked him about the price, he said that I had already paid for it. I did not really understand what he said at that point but still left him a $50 bill just for his amusing and rather stupid story. It was not until a few nights ago that I realized what this ring was capable of.

"A few nights ago, I got a call from the airline that my ticket had been canceled. There was no way for me to fly back because of the weather. I told them that I needed to get back at all costs, to which they responded that the only way for me to come back was if I wished for the weather to clear."

"Oh, Dad. Please don't tell me you wished for the weather to be clear again, and the ring granted that wish for you," Rachel scoffed as she decided to load the dishwasher.

"I wish it were as simple, honey. But there's more to it. I did wish for the weather to clear, and yes, the weather cleared the next morning. But during that flight, our plane almost crashed on a remote island, and guess what? I wished that it stabilized itself in the air and it did. That is what ensured that I landed safely."

Even though Rachel did not believe anything Mike was saying, Jimmy, on the other hand, was a lot more convinced. Before he could say anything, Mike asked him to put the ring on and make a wish, any wish.

Jimmy excitedly did just that. He put the ring on, and he wished to pass his exam, the same exam he knew he would flunk because he did not even bother going to a single glass.

That conversation ended abruptly when Rachel got annoyed and asked Jimmy to go to bed. Mike did not bother asking for the ring back and all three of them went to bed.

***

Jimmy could not fall asleep. He was excited and spent the entire time examining the ring, trying to find more about it on the internet, but all of it was in vain.

Sure, he did find some old clippings from various sources talking about a ring that holds the power to grant wishes, but nothing was concrete. He decided to just let it go.

The next morning, Jimmy decided to wake the whole house up because someone at his school had told him that he had not only passed the exams, but he got the highest scores in the school.

Rachel, on the other hand, did not believe Jimmy for the simplest reason that the result was not going to come out until twelve, and they were still five hours away from it.

She listened to Jimmy being a nuisance and decided to start the day regardless. Jimmy was all over the place with excitement and decided to leave for school on time. This surprised Rachel and she looked at Mike and said, "If I'd known a ring would make my son such a good person, I would have bought him one a long time ago."

Mike laughed, looking at Rachel. "Rachel, this is no ordinary ring. This does not come at a price but can demand a heavy toll."

Rachel did not pay much attention because, to her, it was still a fairy tale, and she was still sleepy to pay attention.

The day had passed, and Jimmy called his mother and told her about the results. He did top the class, and everyone was just as shocked as him.

Rachel knew that her son would not be coming home early so she decided to check up on Mike. When she was about to enter Mike's room, she heard him whispering to someone. At first, she thought that Mike was on the phone but then what followed was terrifying.

"Please, I have done what you have asked of me. I could not serve you. But the boy will. He is young: you can claim his soul or his life, but please don't hurt my daughter. I want her to live."

Rachel was disturbed hearing this, and instead of knocking, she barged into the room and saw Mike sitting on the floor, covered in tears.

She inquired what the conversation was about. Mike told her that he had been having nightmares and visions of this force that wanted to give people what they wanted but, at the same time, take something from them in return.

"Kind of like a rabbit's foot," said Rachel as she tried to call Jimmy and tell him not to do anything with the ring.

Mike couldn't stop crying and told Rachel that the most important part of the story he told them about the ring was that the young man who gave Mike the ring also told him about the ring's dark past and how it had claimed many lives before. The lives of Dutch and John, Valinora, and Lyam... all were claimed by this ring.

Trying to break the curse and save his own life, Mike had handed the ring to Jimmy. Being under the assumption that a kid like him would never believe it, and that would not only mitigate this curse but would also allow the ring to go away from Mike forever.

This story freaked Rachel out even more, and she called Jimmy again and again, but there was no response. She called his school, and they told her that Jimmy had left a few hours ago.

Rachel was reduced to tears and distress at this point when she heard the doorbell. She ran to the door, assuming it was Jimmy, but instead she was faced by two police officers.

"Ms. Rachel, are you the mother of one Jimmy."

"Yes, that's me, officer. Is everything okay?"

"I'm afraid we cannot talk here. You will have to come down to the precinct with us."

Rachel grabbed her keys and went to the precinct with the two police officers. While Mike was in the corridor with a strange, sinister calmness around me. He figured that the ring had claimed its victim, and he was safe. And so was his daughter. Or at least that is what he thought ... because Rachel never returned that night or the next day.

She never came back.

***

Months had passed, and Mike was trying to settle some documents so he could move away from this place when he got a phone call.

"Am I speaking to Mike? Sir, I have to tell you that a few months ago, your grandson was viciously murdered in an alley over what seemed like petty theft. However, that night, we found out that the same people who killed Jimmy came after his mother, too. Your daughter stopped by a shop to get some flowers when she was brutally murdered. We could not apprehend the killers, but we do know it was the same group. Rest assured; we have our best team looking for them. Could you please come to the..."

Before the voice could talk further, Mike dropped the phone and smashed it into the wall. He realized that the ring truly was sinister and had managed to claim not just one but two victims.

He was devastated, but a strange calm was around him because he knew that the ring would not come for him again.

He had nothing left.

Scarlet Night

For most of his life, Jesse never really did anything that would make him stand out as a person. He spent his entire life wasting away in school and in university. However, the one thing that did stand out about Jesse was just how smart he was. Sure, he might not be book smart, but when it came to street smarts or creativity, he could hardly be beaten at his game and that was what made him popular.

Jesse, despite his best efforts, could not derail his life. At an age when his friends were moving out of their parents' homes and living alone, Jesse was still with his parents. For some reason, his parents did not have a problem.

Similarly, Jesse never had any issues with money. Despite not having a job, he always had everything in his possession. He was always the best-dressed student or the person wherever he would go. Despite all the glitter that his personality exuded, there was a dark secret to Jesse. A secret that no one knew, not even Tess, Jesse's high school sweetheart who'd been with him for the longest time. Both were as close as one could get to each other; one can almost assume that they were bonded by blood. Despite Tess being madly in love with Jesse, she knew everything had to be realistic. That's why every time Jesse would do something wrong, Tess would get mad at him. Surely, Jesse knew how to talk to her and cool her down, but their relationship was thriving.

Until now all of this had been a secret. Someone investigating found the power and found people owning the rings had died.

Jesse never told anyone about it because he was afraid that he would be accused of stealing because how else does a teenager come into possession of something that glimmers and shines brighter than all the precious metals combined?

The ring had magical powers. It would grant the wearer any wish that they would ask for. At the same time, it would take away something from them. Since Jesse never really had anything to lose, the ring was bound to Jesse's soul, and every time he used the ring, a part of his soul would get lost without his knowledge.

Jesse was also very giving. Every time someone would come to him for something, he would make sure that they had it.

"Hey Jesse, can you lend me a few hundred bucks? I will return the money to you as soon as I can," claimed one of these friends, and Jesse, without a second thought, handed him the money.

No one knew where the money came from. Only Jesse and his dog Teacup were aware of it. Teacup knew he would never leave Jesse's side, and he'd seen Jesse talk to the ring every time he needed something.

Jesse did not know much about Teacup; one day the dog just appeared at his door, and he took him in. After all, how could you turn away a Labrador puppy, right? The one peculiar thing that Jesse noticed about Teacup was just how he would get excited every time he would take out the ring and talk to it.

"You ready for some magic, Teacup?" Jesse exclaimed as he pulled out the ring from his drawer and put it on his finger. Teacup just looked at Jesse in awe and knew something about the ring was wrong. Since he was just a dog, Jesse did not pay much attention, in the first place, and he never bothered Teacup, either. What was Jesse going to do?

Time kept passing and Jesse did not stop using the ring. Soon, he started realizing that he could not feel anything. Physical, emotional, or mental. Jesse had no feelings left. He would look at himself in the mirror and would realize that the person staring back at him was nothing more than an entity.

On the contrary, Teacup had started moving away from Jesse as well. It was as if he realized that Jesse no longer had the same feelings for him as before, and this only worried the dog. After all, he was still a dog who wanted his owner to feel good.

One night while Jessie was in his room trying to figure out what he needed to do the next day, Teacup came to him for affection. Jessie, not being able to feel anything, shunned Teacup away. Teacup, being just an innocent dog, kept coming back to Jessie for some affection.

Jessie, not knowing what to do with the dog, locked him outside the house and proceeded to go back in and put on the ring. "Can this dog please shut up and go away?" said Jessie as he tried to figure out what needed to be done.

The ring flashed again, this time, however, letting a scarlet shine that filled the room and left Jessie startled. Jessie ran down and opened the front door, and there was no sign of Teacup or anything else, for that matter; the dog had dug his way out of the yard and left Jesse alone.

However, on the floor, there was another ring, much like the ring that Jessie had. This one did not have the glimmer. It was a dull, beaten-up ring. Jessie picked it up, examined it closely, and decided to put it on. After putting it on, he realized that the ring was not really doing anything. It felt and looked like a useless ring; Jesse even tried to ask something from this ring but all in vain. He decided to take it off and throw it away, and as he started taking the ring off, he realized that it would simply not come off. Instead, blood poured out of his fingers from tiny spikes in the ring. The spikes cut into his skin at his wrist, and he screamed.

Soon, Jessie's body was bloodless, but the second ring, the ring that Jesse picked up soaked all the blood and suddenly, it looked like the most beautiful ring, with gleaming silver and intricate scarlet inlays. Jesse's lifeless body lay on the floor, with two distinctively beautiful rings, with no one to explain what had happened.

The power of the combined rings was buried with Jessie until one day legend and grave robbers would come along.
The whole sky was scarlet.

www.ingramcontent.com/pod-product-compliance
Lightning Source LLC
Chambersburg PA
CBHW071224130626
46555CB00004B/1829